Black Pearl
ponies

The BLACK PEARL PONIES series:

1: Red Star

2: Wildflower

3: Miss Molly

4: Stormcloud

5: Snickers

6: Ghost Horse

RED STAR

JENNY OLDFIELD

Illustrated by
JOHN GREEN

Hodder
Children's
Books

A division of Hachette Children's Books

Text copyright © 2011 Jenny Oldfield
Illustrations copyright © 2011 John Green

First published in Great Britain in 2011
by Hodder Children's Books

The rights of Jenny Oldfield and John Green to be identified as the
Author and Illustrator of the Work respectively have been asserted by them in
accordance with the Copyright, Designs and Patents Act 1988.

1

A Catalogue record for this book is available from the British Library

ISBN: 978 0 340 99892 2

Printed and bound in the UK by
CPI Bookmarque Ltd, Croydon, CR0 4TD

The paper and board used in this paperback by
Hodder Children's Books are natural recyclable products made from wood
grown in sustainable forests. The manufacturing processes conform to the
environmental regulations of the country of origin.

Hodder Children's Books
A division of Hachette Children's Books
338 Euston Road, London NW1 3BH
An Hachette UK company
www.hachette.co.uk

*Once more with thanks to the Foster family
and all my friends at Lost Valley Ranch, and this
time with special thanks to Katie Foster, horse
trainer and all-round equine expert.*

CHAPTER ONE

'Go, Keira!' Brooke Lucas sat on the arena fence watching her kid sister ride her pony. 'Go, Red Star – yeah!'

Keira sat deep in the saddle. She loped Red Star around the arena then reined him back in a sliding stop.

'Hey!' Brooke spluttered as the pony dug in his hooves and the dust rose into her face. 'Not so close, puh-lease!' Keira grinned. She leaned forward to pat Red Star's neck. 'Good job!' she told him. 'Now how about a couple of spins in the centre of the arena?'

'And how about you untack your pony and help in the feed stalls?' a voice broke in. It was Keira and Brooke's mother, Allyson, calling to the girls as she walked out of the barn. 'Save the pirouettes for later!'

Grinning again, Keira guided Red Star through the gate into the corral. The late afternoon sun was hot on her face, though long shadows fell across the ground as she tethered him to the nearest rail. 'Now, eat,' she told him. 'You worked hard back there so you get extra feed!'

Brooke helped her sister to unbuckle Red Star's cinch and carry the heavy saddle into the tack

room. 'I already fed Annie and put her out in the meadow,' she explained about her own pony before scooting off towards the house. 'Now I'm out of here – I have school work to finish.'

'So you eat with the big guys,' Keira told her pony as she led him towards the row of wooden feed stalls. She spotted her mom's dark bay horse, Captain, and her dad's tall grey mare, Misty, already chomping at the grain pellets in their mangers. 'We need to feed you and build up your strength ready for the competition in Sheriton County next month.'

'It's non-stop work around here.' Allyson faked a sigh as she tipped grain into Red Star's stall. Really she loved every minute of the daily routine at Black Pearl Ranch. 'You know your dad has gone to pick

4

up a new pony? He's called Tornado.'

'Cool!' Keira loved the noisy way horses ate, their big teeth chomping on the grain. She stared happily at Red Star, studying the pattern of red-brown flecks which covered his body, standing out against a light grey background. 'What's the story with Tornado?'

'He belongs to the Masons in Norton County. The daughter, Meredith, is having some problems with him. They've hired your dad to fix him.' Allyson looked up and noticed a big truck heading down the steep track. 'Here comes the new guy with the hay!' she exclaimed, dashing off to meet it.

Keira ignored the squeal of brakes and the bump and rattle of the truck over the rough surface. 'Tornado, huh? You hear that, Red Star? You're about to meet another problem pony!'

Red Star raised his head, curled back his lips and snickered. Then he made a sneaky move along the manger to snatch a mouthful of grain from Misty's stall. *You said I deserved extra feed!* he seemed to say.

'Quit that!' Keira laughed. She found it hard to be tough on him, he looked so cute and loveable.

In any case, there was a lot going on. Matt Brown, the new hay man, was busy unloading bales into the barn, and a bright red SUV was following him down the track.

'That'll be Owen Mason,' Allyson predicted as she hurried by. 'Your dad must be close behind.'

'OK, Red Star, it's time for your beauty treatment.' Untying him, Keira led him back to the corral and went to fetch a brush and comb. When she got back, she could hear her mom talking to Owen Mason.

'Tornado has some bad habits,' he was telling Allyson. 'If you get too close behind him, he has a real nasty kick. Plus, my daughter, Meredith, she's not a strong kid and this pony will ride through any bit you put in his mouth.'

'Jacob will handle him, no problem,' Allyson assured Mason. 'That's what we do here at Black Pearl Ranch – we train out those bad habits.'

'Now that pony over there …' the visitor turned to look at Red Star, '… he's real nice-looking. I guess you don't have those problems with him.'

Allyson smiled. 'We've had Red Star a long time. As a matter of fact, he was born here.'

On the same day as me! Keira glowed with pleasure as she combed through her pony's silky white mane. *We share the same birthday!*

For as far back as she could remember Red Star had been the biggest thing in her life. He'd been the first pony her mom had ever put her on, when she was one and a half years old. A little later, her dad had made her a special junior saddle with Red Star's name tooled into the leather in fancy letters.

'Red Star and Keira have grown up together,' Allyson told the visitor. 'She's training him to compete in junior reining events.'

'Cute,' Mr Mason noted, turning to look at the trailer easing its way down the dusty track. 'That's part of our problem – we have no history for Meredith's pony. I wish we'd known more about

Tornado before we went ahead and spent good money on him.'

Keira had time to walk Red Star down to the meadow before her dad finally pulled the trailer into the yard. Red Star danced and pranced at her side, eager to get out onto the grass with Brooke's pony, Annie. When she took off his head collar, he gave a buck of pure pleasure and cantered off.

'Tornado hates to travel in the trailer,' Owen Mason was warning Jacob Lucas when Keira got back to the yard. 'He sweats up and kicks out – you take care when you open that door!'

Is there any single thing he likes about this pony? Keira wondered. She frowned and bit her lip at the sound of Tornado whinnying from inside the trailer, expecting the worst.

Her dad slid the bolts and opened the door. The pony inside the trailer stamped his hooves against the metal floor.

'Stand back,' Owen Mason warned again.

But Keira's dad stepped confidently into the trailer. 'Easy, boy,' he murmured.

There was silence in the yard as he untied the pony to lead him out.

That's so not good! Keira thought as she caught her first glimpse of Tornado. He was a brown and white paint – mainly white, but with brown patches across his back and withers – strongly built and with a handsome head. His whole body was dark with sweat and foam had formed at the corners of his mouth. He flattened his ears and rolled his eyes as he stood framed by the trailer doorway.

'Good job, good boy,' Jacob soothed, easing Tornado out into the open air.

The pony stepped down awkwardly, ears still flat against his head. He jerked his head sideways, pulling the lead rope taut.

'What did I tell you?' Mr Mason muttered. 'This pony doesn't travel well.'

'Easy,' Jacob insisted, waiting patiently for the

new arrival to settle down.

Tornado whinnied and kept on pulling on his rope. He pranced across the yard towards the barn.

While Keira's dad calmed the pony, her mom went to work on his owner. 'Leave Tornado with us for a week, Owen, and you won't recognise him. Jacob will take him right back to the start and fix him, no problem.'

'You think you can stop him from taking off with Meredith?'

Allyson nodded. 'Keira here will help her dad. She'll hop up in the saddle for a couple of test rides. I guess she's around the same size as your daughter?'

Mr Mason nodded. 'But Tornado is a real handful, believe me.'

He doesn't look so bad, Keira thought. By now her dad was walking the pony steadily around the yard, right by the hay wagon parked up alongside the barn. *Uh-oh, I spoke too soon!*

Just then Matt Brown jumped down from the back of the wagon with the last bale of hay. He spooked Tornado, who pulled free from her dad and started to gallop straight at the sturdy corral fence.

'Watch out – he's going to bust right through!' Owen Mason yelled.

The pony seemed dead set on crashing into the fence.

'No, he plans to jump it!' Keira cried.

Sure enough, Tornado rested back on his haunches and cleared the fence with a mighty leap, almost crashing into the nearest tethering rail. He swerved and galloped on, only sliding to a stop by the tack room door.

'Crazy pony!' Owen Mason shook his head while Keira and her mom ran to help Tornado.

'Easy, boy!' Keira whispered as Allyson cornered him. 'No one's going to hurt you.'

Tornado shook and trembled. He breathed hard, his sides heaving in and out.

Allyson edged in closer. 'That's good, Keira – he's paying attention to you!'

'We're here to help,' Keira explained, watching

every move the pony made. She noticed his ears flick towards her and his eyes stay fixed on her. 'We know you had a hard time back there in the trailer. Just take it easy, huh!'

At last her mom was close enough to grab hold of Tornado's trailing lead rope. She reached forward and held it tight while Keira opened the gate into the feed stalls.

'Good idea,' Allyson nodded. 'We'll put him in there, give him time to unwind.'

'Take it easy,' Keira murmured again.

Tornado seemed to respond. He stopped pulling at his rope and let himself be led into the nearest stall. Soon he was safely tethered, gazing into the distance at the red sun sinking fast over the jagged range of the Black Pearl Mountains.

'And now it's time for supper!' Allyson said with a satisfied grin. 'Hash browns, ham and eggs. Come on, Keira – let's get over to the house before the others eat it all!'

CHAPTER TWO

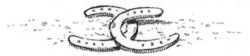

Next morning Keira was up soon after dawn. She scrambled into her jeans and shirt, eager to get on with the day.

In her mind she ran through a list of early chores:

* walk out to the meadow and bring the ponies into the corral

* groom Red Star

* clean his tack

* sweep out tack room

* count head collars and lead ropes.

It was her Saturday routine, and she could already hear Brooke's footsteps on the stairs down into the kitchen. She ran a brush through her red-gold hair and quickly tied it back. Then she threw on a jacket, pulled on her boots and dashed downstairs.

'Early breakfast to-go!' her dad said, handing her a chunky bacon sandwich as she headed for the back door.

Keira thanked him, let the door slam behind her, grabbed a head collar from the tack room then sprinted to catch up with Brooke. 'Let's visit Tornado – see how he got through the night,' she suggested.

So the girls detoured down the side of the barn to

check on the new pony.

They found him standing quietly in the stable they used in the spring for brood mares. The two mares and their foals were already out in the meadow, so the problem pony had the place to himself.

'It looks like he's settled in,' Brooke said with a smile.

Tornado raised his head to them and gave a soft snort, pushing his nose into Keira's empty hand.

'Look – I haven't got anything for you to eat!' Keira laughed. She was glad to see Tornado calm and relaxed. 'Wait here while we fetch the others in from the meadow, then maybe you can make some new friends.'

She and Brooke left the barn and hurried on to

the dew-covered meadow where Red Star and Annie stood at the gate to greet them. In the distance, Captain and Misty grazed happily alongside the two mares and their cute, gangly foals.

'Hey, Red Star, hey, Annie!' Quickly Keira and Brooke slipped the head collars onto their ponies and led them along the side of the creek, back towards the ranch. The sun had risen over the mountains to the east, turning the sky from cool grey to hot pink. By the time they reached the corral, their dad had brought Tornado out of the stables, tethered him to a rail in the corral and was busy brushing him from head to tail.

'Hey, handsome!' Keira said, tethering Red Star next to him. She got busy with her own brush and comb, taking the dust and dirt out of Red Star's speckled coat. Brooke did likewise with Annie. Soon all three ponies were gleaming.

'So now I work with Tornado in the arena,' Jacob explained. He was dressed in a pale blue shirt, jeans and well-worn cowboy boots. His dark, wavy hair was freshly washed.

'Is it OK if I skip my tack room chores to come and watch?' Keira asked.

'Chores first, watch your dad second,' Allyson insisted from the door of the tack room. 'Jacob, Owen Mason called to say he plans to be here early!'

Keira's dad nodded. 'No problem. He'll see me working on join-up before I get up in the saddle.'

Keira left Red Star tethered and ran to finish her

chores in record time.

'Mom says we get some down-time later today,' Brooke told her as she tidied a shelf. 'Let's ride out along the Jeep Road.'

'Cool!' Keira agreed, hurrying out to watch Tornado in the arena.

Jacob was already hard at work with the pony. He held a length of rope in one hand, snaking it out along the ground behind Tornado so that he loped on ahead of it. Every time Jacob wriggled the rope in the dirt, the pony picked up speed to flee ahead, until eventually he was tired and he lowered his head so that his nose almost touched the ground.

'OK, good boy.' Keira's dad let him slow down to a walk. When the pony halted, Jacob stayed in the centre of the arena and waited for him to approach.

Keira loved this moment of join-up. She sat on the fence, watching Tornado decide that his best bet was to quit running and make friends with the guy with the rope. Ponies were smart about this – in the end they always came into the middle of the arena to be stroked and rewarded.

Sure enough, the strong little paint approached Jacob and nuzzled his hand.

'Good job!' Keira breathed. She smiled as

she noticed Owen Mason's SUV bumping down the track. 'How big a surprise will he get when he sees you!'

Her dad patted Tornado's neck then rubbed his nose. 'Hey, Keira – it's time we put a saddle on,' he said.

She ran to the tack room. When she came out carrying Tornado's saddle, her dad was deep in conversation with Mr Mason, with a small, fair-haired girl standing by.

'Hi.' Keira gave the girl a bright smile. 'You must be Meredith. I really like your pony – he's a smart guy.'

Meredith looked back with a worried frown. 'You think so?'

'Yeah. By the way, I'm Keira Lucas. Do you want

to help me put Tornado's saddle and bridle on?'

Meredith's frown stayed put. 'I'll watch you do it, if that's OK.'

'Sure. Let's go.' Leaving the adults to talk, Keira led the way into the arena. She felt Meredith hang back as they drew close to Tornado.

'He won't kick me again, will he?' the newcomer asked. She kept a wary eye on her pony, who stood calmly as Keira slid his saddle over his broad back.

'Why? When did he do that?'

'Last week, in our barn. I came up behind him and he kicked me on the leg.'

'Ouch!' Keira tightened the girth and checked the stirrups. 'That tells you not to come at him from behind. It probably spooked him.' Now it was time to slip the bit in. Keira had done it a million times

– just ease back the corners of the horse's mouth and make him relax his jaw to accept the bar of metal over his tongue.

'Hey, you're good at that,' Meredith murmured. She was around ten years old – the same as Keira, but without Keira's easy-going manner. In fact, she seemed pretty uptight and reserved.

'Here at Black Pearl I get to practise a lot,' Keira grinned. 'How long have you owned Tornado?'

'Three months,' Meredith told her. She didn't go up to him to stroke him and say hi. 'He's my first pony.'

'So you're both on a steep learning curve,' Keira said. 'It's good that you brought Tornado to Black Pearl Ranch – my dad's a great trainer!'

'Thanks, but don't expect miracles,' Jacob

warned as he left Owen Mason's side and came to test Tornado's girth and step into the saddle. Tornado shifted sideways then pranced uneasily.

'Stand clear, Meredith!' Mason warned sharply.

Boy, are these guys jumpy! Keira tried not to judge, but she knew the pony would pick up on their worries. 'Let's watch from a safe distance,' she suggested as she headed for the gate.

Once there was a strong wooden barrier between her and Tornado, Meredith started to relax. She watched closely as Jacob set him into a trot then a lope around the arena. Tornado behaved just like he should – listening to his rider, picking up speed, turning and stopping to order.

'He's so handsome!' Keira admired his brown and white markings, his long, flowing mane and the proud way he held his head.

'I guess,' Meredith murmured.

Meanwhile, her dad started to find faults. 'He loped way too fast around that last bend,' he complained. 'Almost had his rider out of the saddle.'

No way! Keira bit her tongue. Her mom and dad had a rule – never argue with a client!

'And look at him now, the way he's tossing his head – he's fighting for control!'

That's called having a good time! Keira wanted to tell Owen Mason.

They watched Jacob and Tornado lope again then make a flying lead change for a sudden switch of direction.

'Crazy!' Meredith's dad shook his head. 'What

did I tell you? That's one dangerous son of a gun!'

'But …!' He did what Dad was telling him to do!

It was a relief that her mom and sister came along right then. 'Hey, Mr Mason,' Allyson interrupted. 'Your pony's looking good in there.'

'You reckon?' Owen Mason shook his head. 'Did you see the speed he had on that last turn? Even Jacob couldn't hold him back, and he's a strong guy!'

Keira snuck a look at Brooke who raised her eyebrows but said nothing.

Standing close to her father, Meredith had on her worried expression.

Everyone waited for Jacob to walk Tornado over to the group of onlookers.

'I want you to slow that pony right down,' Owen

insisted. 'No rodeo stuff, OK!'

'I hear you.' Keira's dad nodded. His face didn't give anything away.

'Walking and trotting – no loping. You make this pony solid as a rock for my daughter – you hear?'

Keira noticed Owen Mason turning red in the face, while Meredith shrank into the background.

Mason stormed on. 'I want him one hundred per

cent reliable – no loping, no bucking, no kicking!'

'Gotcha,' Jacob said.

Mason drew his car keys from his jeans pocket and turned towards his car. 'You have one week!' he reminded them. 'One week to turn this little spitfire into a trouble-free ride for my girl!'

CHAPTER THREE

'No way is Tornado the problem!' Keira confided in Brooke as they rode the Jeep Road.

'I agree. Mr Mason was way too hard on him.' Brooke steered Annie wide of a tall pine tree, ducking under a low branch as she rode past. Together the girls and their ponies headed away from the ranch up into the hills.

They were silent for a while, listening to the

steady crunch of hooves on the sandy ground, looking out for wildlife such as mule deer or coyote. Then Keira went back to the same topic. 'I can't see anything wrong with that pony. He's pretty near perfect, actually.'

'Yeah, for a three-year-old he's doing great.' Brooke let Keira and Red Star lead the way along a narrow ledge.

'Only three!' Keira was surprised. 'How come a novice rider gets such a young horse?'

'Because!' Brooke sighed. She wished Keira would cool down and enjoy the ride. 'Let Mom and Dad deal with it, OK?'

'I didn't like the way Mr Mason talked about Tornado,' Keira grumbled. 'He called him a spitfire – did you hear?'

'Yeah, but don't worry – ponies don't understand English!' Brooke laughed as she set Annie at a lope up a long, smooth stretch of track.

'I'm not so sure.' Keira followed on Red Star. With the wind in her hair and the ground flashing by, she forgot her worries about the little paint pony back in the corral.

At the top of the hill they paused to give Annie and Red Star a break.

'Uh-oh!' Brooke saw a movement beside a big, domed rock to their left. She put her finger to her lips, warning Keira to stay quiet.

Keira stared at the deep shadow cast by Dolphin Rock. 'Yep,' she breathed. She spotted an animal larger than a deer, partly hidden by bushes. When it saw them, it raised its head and let out a sad moo.

At the same moment, a small calf ran out from behind the rock. 'Hey, you shouldn't be on our land,' Keira told the momma cow and baby. 'My bet is that you belong at the Walters' place!'

'Yeah – the Three Horseshoes did a cattle round-up earlier this week. They brought all the cows in before the first snowfall.' Brooke rode slowly towards the runaways. 'Now don't spook. We're on your side!'

Keira laughed at the calf's attempt to hide behind his big black and white mom. 'Hey, Red Star, we get to drive cattle!' Riding wide of the rock, she planned on coming up behind the cow and calf to drive them towards Brooke and Annie.

'Cool!' Brooke called. 'Nice and easy does it.' Before the cattle knew it they were caught in a pincer movement between the two riders. 'Now all we have to do is get them in one piece down to the Three Horseshoes!'

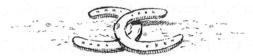

Driving cattle on a warm September afternoon was thirsty work.

'Yip!' Keira called as the cows trudged down into the neighbouring valley. The telltale brand of three linked horseshoes stood out clearly on the momma's broad rear end. 'Yip, cows, yip!'

The mother would drag along with her head down then would suddenly break away in a mad rush into the bushes, her calf crashing along at her heels. Brooke or Keira would ride after them and quickly get them back on track.

'Yip!' Brooke urged them on, letting Annie nip at them with her teeth to hurry them along.

It took all of two hours to get them downhill through the aspens and along the creek to the Walters' ranch.

'Hey girls, good job!' Tom Walters was out in the yard with Matt Brown and the hay wagon. He was the first to spot them driving his cows home. 'I've been out looking for that pair for three whole days!'

The rancher opened a gate for the runaways, calling to his son, Reed, to lend a hand.

Keira and Brooke knew twelve-year-old Reed from way back. They went to school with him and hung out together. He was the sort who didn't say much, but was always smiling. Right now he took over from the girls and shooed the cow and calf towards the creek to drink. Meanwhile, Tom Walters gave instructions to Matt about where to stack the hay bales then invited Brooke and Keira into the house.

'Where did you find my cows?' Tom wanted to know.

'By Dolphin Rock,' Brooke told him. 'There's a stretch of fence down.'

'Reed and I will ride up there to fix it tomorrow,' Tom promised as Keira gulped down a glass of iced water. 'Thirsty work,' he smiled. 'You want me to trailer you back home?'

'No, we're good, thanks.' Brooke decided that she and Keira would ride the Low Ridge route back. 'Reed, do you want to ride with us?'

He nodded. In less than five minutes he'd saddled

his pony, Duke, and was waiting for them by the cattle guard.

Keira's legs felt weary as she sat back in the saddle. 'Go easy on me, Red Star,' she sighed. But she'd loved every minute of the cattle drive and couldn't wait to tell her mom and dad. As soon as they got on to Low Ridge, her body was warmed up again and she was yackety-yacking with Reed.

'You know something? My dad is working with a so-called problem pony named Tornado. According to the owners, this guy bucks and kicks, rears and does all sorts of stuff. But the truth is – the pony is cool. It's the owners who have all the problems!'

Reed Walters rode with Keira and Brooke to the Black Pearl boundary fence, where he said goodbye.

Brooke turned in the saddle to watch him and Duke head back home. 'You didn't let Reed say two words!' she complained to Keira. 'You're so busy telling him that Tornado does this and Tornado does that, blah-blah …'

'Oops!' Keira knew that she could be a pain sometimes. 'Reed did seem interested though.'

'How could you tell?' Brooke laughed.

'He looked interested!'

The girls rode slowly on, glad to reach the meadow with the brood mares, Ruby and Willow, and their two so-far unnamed foals. At the far gate they saw their mom returning Misty and Captain to the lush green grass after an afternoon's work in the arena. Allyson waited for the girls to join her.

Keira trotted Red Star ahead of Annie. 'Mom, guess what! We found a cow and calf from Three Horseshoes up by Dolphin Rock ...' A serious look on her mom's face suddenly stopped her. 'What is it? What's wrong?'

'It's OK, probably nothing,' Allyson said with a shake of her head. Dressed in T-shirt, jeans and boots, she was slight and small, and with her reddish-blonde hair tied back, it was easy to see where Keira got her looks. 'Your dad took a phone call, that's all.'

'Who from?' Setting off towards the house at a walk, Brooke and Keira rode on either side of their mom.

'From Owen Mason,' Allyson told them quietly.

'About Tornado?' Keira felt a knot in her stomach. This definitely wasn't good news.

Her mom nodded. 'He said he'd been thinking about the way Tornado acted earlier today.'

'But!'

'Keira!' Brooke warned her to stay quiet.

'Owen Mason seems pretty convinced that Tornado's problem is too bad for your dad to fix.'

'But!' Keira gasped again.

'So he broke the news that they may put the pony up for sale,' Allyson said. 'He won't make a final decision until the end of next week, but Jacob guesses that it'll happen. The Masons have already given up on Tornado, end of story.'

CHAPTER FOUR

That night Tornado stayed out in the meadow with Red Star and the other Black Pearl ponies. He grazed peacefully under the stars and when Keira went out there early, she couldn't help but think all over again how wrong Owen Mason was.

'You know something, Red Star?' She sighed as she gave her pony a morning hug. 'I think maybe it's a good idea for the Masons to sell Tornado!'

Red Star nuzzled her hand. He walked by her side all the way up to Tornado, who raised his head and snickered.

'You could go to owners who like you just the way you are,' she explained. 'People who know how to ride and look after a pony!'

'But then what about the work I'm putting in?' Keira's dad had been in the meadow all along. He popped up from behind Misty, ready to tease Keira for having a conversation with the ponies. 'Hey, Tornado – will Owen Mason pay me what he owes me, come the end of the week?'

'Oops, I never thought of that,' Keira admitted. 'So maybe the Masons should keep you after all.'

'And we should work on Meredith when she pays her next visit,' her dad agreed. 'Help her gain a little confidence, teach her how to love her pony.'

Keira nodded. 'Good idea. Then Mr Mason will agree not to sell.'

Jacob smiled as he fastened a head collar onto Misty and began to walk her out of the meadow. 'It's going to be tough,' he admitted. 'The kid is a wreck whenever Tornado comes near. And her dad isn't exactly Mister Patience.'

'But we can do it!' Keira called after him. 'We get Meredith to love Tornado and you get your pay cheque at the end of the week!'

Life at Black Pearl Ranch was nowhere near picture-book perfect. Keira knew how her parents fought to make the horse and pony training

business pay. The prize money that her mom and Captain won at reining competitions helped, but the family was a long way short of being able to relax.

'I hope we never have to go back to live in the city.' As usual, Keira shared her worries with Red Star. It was 9.00 a.m. on Sunday morning and she had him in the corral, grooming him and giving him his beauty treatments before she took him into the arena.

All her life she'd lived the dream out here at the ranch, but it was only the year before she was born that her parents had agreed to take it on. That was when Jacob's uncle, Bob Lucas, had retired.

'Black Pearl Ranch is the most magical place you could ever wish to be,' Uncle Bob had told Jacob and Allyson. 'It's named after the shine and shimmer of the mountains at dawn – they glow like black pearls, and there's nothing in this world more beautiful. But don't be fooled – it's a hard life training colts and fillies. You work 24/7 to put food on the table for your family, and you've got to be head and shoulders better than the rest, even to do that.'

It had proved true. As Brooke and Keira were growing up, their dad and mom had worked hard and given up all luxuries. Even now, every cent they earned counted.

'Which is why we have to hope that Mr Mason pays Dad what he owes,' Keira sighed, standing back to admire Red Star. 'And why I have to work on Meredith next time she visits.'

Red Star sighed too. He had such a wise look in his big brown eyes that Keira was sure he'd taken on board every word she said. And how gorgeous was he! His white mane and tail shone like silk, the strawberry roan flecks on his white coat seemed to dance in the sunlight.

She went into the tack room to fetch his saddle, looking forward to the session they were about to put in. They would work in the arena on sliding stops and spins, leading up to flying lead changes. With luck, Keira's mom would be there to give them expert advice.

'We have the Sheriton County junior competition coming up,' Keira reminded Red Star as she tightened his cinch and checked his bridle. 'October 6th. We have to be ready by then.'

The pony pricked up his ears and she sprang into the saddle. A quick warm-up followed, then they were trotting and loping, rehearsing their sliding stops across the centre of the arena.

'Good, but rein him back a little earlier,' Allyson called. She stood at the gate watching Keira's every move. 'Get him to tuck his hindquarters in about one third of the way across – good, that's great!'

'Good boy, Red Star!' Keira leaned forward to pat him. Then she neck reined him to lope in a clockwise direction around the arena. 'Again,' she whispered, reining him towards the centre and going into another stop. Red Star dug in his back feet, slid about ten metres and raised a cloud of dust.

'Now try a spin,' Allyson called. 'Rein him to the

51

right and put on the pressure with your left leg. Stay upright in the saddle!'

Keira followed instructions. Straight away Red Star knew what was expected of him and he turned brilliantly – slowly at first then faster, so that the whole world seemed to spin.

'Good – keep him on the spot, don't let him drift!'

Keira sat perfectly still, her left leg pressed against Red Star's side.

'Enough. Ease off,' Allyson instructed.

Keira took off the pressure and relaxed the reins. Again he did exactly what she told him.

'Perfect,' her mom told them, turning away from the gate and heading off towards the barn.

'You hear that?' Keira jumped down from the saddle and threw her arms around Red Star's neck.

'You didn't put a foot wrong.'

Red Star snickered then nuzzled her cheek. He liked this kind of compliment.

Keira smiled and stood back. 'Jeez, I love you,

Red Star. Mom's right – you're totally perfect!'

'So, are you and Red Star ready for Sheriton?' Brooke asked Keira over lunch.

The whole family sat in the kitchen enjoying a

meal of pizza and salad.

'Are we ready?' Keira asked her mom.

'Pretty near,' Allyson said. 'There's still a little work to do on lead changes.'

'How about you and Annie?' Keira asked Brooke.

'We don't plan on entering this year.' Though she was a talented rider, Brooke happily admitted that she wasn't great in competitions. 'I have a school camp that weekend. But I'll be backing you and Red Star, thinking of you going out there and taking first prize.'

'We hope!' Unlike her sister, Keira loved to compete. She liked the thrill of it – the build-up to her turn, watching the other riders and knowing she and Red Star had to put in the performance of their lives if they wanted to win. The night before the contest she would lie awake rehearsing every last move of their routine in her head.

'OK, so who wants to work with me on Tornado this afternoon?' Jacob got up from the table and began to clear the plates.

Keira shot up to join him.

Her dad grinned. 'I guess I didn't even need to ask!'

She was out of the house ahead of him, grabbing a lead rope and sprinting off towards the meadow. She spotted Annie and Misty close to the gate, then Captain, Tornado and the brood mares plus their foals down by the creek. 'Huh,' she muttered, pushing the gate open. It was off the latch, swinging free. She looked around the meadow. 'Do you see Red Star?' she asked her dad in a worried voice.

'Is he in the willows?' Jacob knew that the ponies sometimes strayed amongst the bushes by the water. Once in a while they got themselves stuck in there.

So Keira ran down to the water. 'Red Star, where are you?' she called, expecting any moment

to hear her pony's feet splashing through the stream and trampling through the brush, to see his flecked face and shiny white mane emerge from the cloud of golden leaves.

But it didn't happen. And the gate had been left open. 'He's not here,' she called to her dad. She ran back up the slope with sudden fear in her heart. 'Dad, what are we going to do? Red Star went walkabout!'

CHAPTER FIVE

'Brooke, did you leave the gate open?' Keira ran into the house, her head in a whirl. 'Before you came in for lunch, were you out in the meadow?'

'No way.' Brooke was totally sure. 'I don't go around leaving gates open so ponies can escape.'

'OK, girls – stay calm.' Allyson knew this was a serious situation. She listened hard as Jacob arrived to confirm that Red Star was missing. 'We need to set up a search party. Brooke, you go check the gate by the cattle guard on the Jeep Road. I'll drive up the track to check the main gate.'

'What about me?' Keira pleaded. She felt sick to her stomach, desperately trying to figure out which direction Red Star might have taken.

'You come with me,' her dad suggested. 'We'll look in the barn and the feed stalls. You know how sneaky he is – maybe he's looking for extra grain.'

So Keira and Jacob hurried across the yard. They searched the big barn, calling Red Star's name.

'He's not here,' Keira sighed. Hay bales were stacked high to the roof, leaving only a narrow central aisle leading to the locked grain store. 'He can't be – there's no place he could hide.'

Her dad backtracked and went to look in the row

of feed stalls. 'Not here either,' he reported. 'And nothing's been disturbed.'

'What are we going to do?' Keira wailed. If only her heart would stop thumping against her ribs, she might be able to figure out a plan.

'Don't panic.' Jacob thought for her. 'I bet your mom finds him up by the main gate, watching for visitors. You know what a friendly little guy he is.'

'That's the problem. Red Star trusts everybody. What if he got friendly with the wrong person?' A dozen fears flicked through Keira's mind. 'Or maybe he bushwhacked across country and fell down a deep hole, or over the edge of a cliff. Or else he got trapped down a gulley and can't make his way out. Dad, there are coyotes out there, and bears ...!'

'I said, don't panic,' her dad insisted. He saw Allyson driving back down the track and waited for her to jump out of the car.

'Nothing,' she told them quietly. 'But the gate's closed. No way did Red Star leave by that route.'

'That's good,' Jacob said firmly. 'So now we drive up the Jeep Road, see what Brooke discovered.'

All three got in the car and drove the rough track.

Halfway up the hill towards Dolphin Rock they met Brooke running back towards them.

'Did you find him?' Keira yelled through the open window.

Brooke shook her head. 'He's

not at the cattle guard. But you know the gap where the cows got through yesterday? Well, the fence is still down.'

'But Tom Walters told us they'd fix it!' Another picture flashed into Keira's head – of Red Star enjoying his freedom and loping up the trail, finding the hole in the fence, making good his escape. From there he could have headed off in any direction.

'Well, they haven't fixed it yet,' Brooke gasped. She'd run a long way and was out of breath. 'You're sure Red Star's not hanging out in the barn?'

Their dad shook his head. 'A pony is pretty hard to miss. If he was still close to the ranch we'd have found him by now.'

Keira's heart raced. She turned to Allyson. 'Mom, what next?'

'We go back and saddle some horses,' her mom decided. 'We carry on looking, this time on horseback.'

To Keira every minute that passed felt like an age. It seemed to take hours to fetch the horses in from the meadow and saddle them up, yet when she looked at her watch it was only 2.30 p.m.

'Who do you want to ride – Misty or Tornado?' her dad asked her as they got ready to leave the corral.

'Take Misty.' Her mom decided for her. 'Tornado is our client's horse. Your dad should ride him.'

So Keira used the mounting block to climb onto Misty's back. The grey mare was over sixteen hands high, but gentle. No one doubted that she would take good care of Keira.

They set off together up the Jeep Road, spreading out when they reached Dolphin Rock. Jacob and Brooke rode north, deep into the pine forest, scanning the hillsides for any sign of Keira's lost pony – fresh hoofprints or droppings – anything that would give them a clue. Meanwhile, Allyson and Keira rode west, through the gap in the razor wire fence, down into Three Horseshoes territory.

'What if Red Star gets scared, out here all by himself?' Keira still ran through all the possibilities. 'He's in places he never went before. Maybe he'll get seriously spooked.'

Allyson went with Captain to search behind every rock and tree. 'Honey, you know yourself – Red Star is a smart pony. He won't do anything that puts him in danger. And horses hate to be alone. I'm betting that the moment Red Star spotted the Walters' place, he headed down there to join their horses.'

Keira nodded. For the first time she felt a glimmer of hope. 'I'll go on ahead,' she told her mom. 'You search up here amongst the aspens while I ride down to the ranch.'

'You take care,' Allyson warned. She picked up and followed a set of hoofprints which cut across the hillside. Soon she and Captain disappeared amongst the fiery red autumn trees.

Keira and Misty hurried downhill, keeping the

Walters' house in sight. As the slope grew steeper, Keira leaned back in the saddle and sent her horse on a zigzag path. She swayed from side to side, feeling Misty's feet sink into the sandy ground. Once in a while the horse would slip and slide a couple of metres before she regained her footing.

'Take it easy!' Keira murmured. 'The last thing we need is for you to get injured.'

The minutes ticked by as they drew nearer to Three Horseshoes ranch house.

'Hey, Keira!' Reed Walters looked up from the processing work he and his dad were doing with the cows and calves in the corral. He seemed pleased to see her.

'What's new?'

'Reed, Red Star got loose from our meadow.

We're all out looking for him. I thought maybe he made his way down here.'

Tom Walters led the way out of the corral, leaving the cows and calves to head off towards the creek.

'No, he didn't show up here,' he told Keira. 'If he had, we'd have made a phone call to all of you at

Black Pearl right away.'

Dejected, Keira turned to Reed. 'We think he got through the hole in the fence – the same one we told you about yesterday.'

Reed frowned then blushed. 'We plan to fix that after we finish here.'

'Too late.' She let him see her anger. 'Red Star's already in trouble'

'Don't get ahead of yourself. We don't know anything for certain yet,' Tom pointed out. 'But I sure am sorry if your pony got free. Reed, you take Duke and ride out with Keira. Give her all the help you can.'

'When did you last see Red Star?' Reed rode alongside Keira as they picked their way across country.

Clouds were gathering over Black Pearl Mountains, so she zipped up her jacket. 'Before lunch,' she replied. 'We worked in the corral then I walked him out to the meadow.'

Reed thought for a while. 'Some ponies figure out how to open gates,' he reminded her. 'Do you reckon Red Star could do that?'

'He never did before. But then, I guess he's smart enough. You're saying maybe no one's to blame for leaving the gate open?'

He nodded. 'I don't want you getting mad at your sister or your parents for no reason.'

'Brooke already said it wasn't her.' Keira frowned. Then she realised she'd been hard on her sister. 'You're right,' she agreed. 'Red Star most likely figured it out for himself.'

Spots of cold rain were starting to fall, the light was growing dim. Misty almost lost her footing on solid rock. She regained her balance then threw back her head and let out a loud neigh. In the distance, a horse answered with a shrill call.

Suddenly alert, Reed flashed a questioning glance at Keira.

She shook her head. 'That's Mom's horse, Captain,' she told him.

They rode on without picking up any signs of a pony's presence. The rain fell with loud splashes onto the tree canopy and bare rocks. There was a roll of thunder way off in the mountains.

Keira shivered. She halted Misty and stared into the far distance. 'What if Red Star stays out alone all night?' she asked Reed.

He shrugged. 'It won't happen.'

'But what if it does? What if Red Star's hurt?'

'You mean – will a bear or a coyote attack a pony?'

Keira caught her breath and nodded. 'Do they ever attack your cattle?'

'Only if the cow's injured or sick.' He spoke so quietly she could hardly hear. They sat side by side, pointing Duke and Misty out towards the wide wilderness, watching the rain. 'I can't lie to you, Keira. It does sometimes happen.'

CHAPTER SIX

Keira and Reed stayed out in the rain until late afternoon. They were soaked through but they found no sign of the missing pony.

'We have to go back,' Reed decided at last. 'It's no good staying out any longer.'

'I can't,' Keira told him. She felt tears well up in her eyes and tried to swallow them back down. 'Not until I find out what happened to Red Star.'

Just then, her dad appeared on the brow of

the hill. He was on foot, leading Tornado, who was limping.

'What happened?' Keira gasped, her mind suddenly torn away from the search.

'He went lame with a stone in his hoof,' Jacob explained, taking off his Stetson and shaking water from the brim. 'It's not serious – maybe a bruise, nothing more. I already picked out the stone. Now I'm walking him back to the ranch.'

Poor Tornado! Keira watched him limp towards them. The sturdy paint pony looked sorry for himself, with his head down and the rain trickling through his mane and down his face. *Nothing's going right for you.*

'It's time for you two to come off the mountain and get dry,' her dad said. 'Allyson and Brooke already went ahead of us.'

'Did anyone pick up any clues?' Reed asked.

Keira hung her head. She already knew what the answer would be.

'Not a thing,' Jacob replied.

They came to a stop by Dolphin Rock for one final look around – up the mountain then over towards the row of pine trees on a ledge overlooking the valley, then back towards the gap in the fence.

'Wait a second!' Keira spotted something she hadn't noticed before. Urging Misty towards the dangerous, coiled-up razor wire, she stared down at the ground. 'Dad, Reed – come over here!'

Reluctantly they joined her.

Keira pointed to tyre tracks in the mud. 'Look!'

Jacob handed Tornado's reins to Reed and knelt to take a closer look. 'Cars don't usually come off the Jeep Road,' he muttered. 'And these are definitely pretty recent.'

'Maybe Dad drove up to fix the fence,' Reed suggested.

Keira shook her head. 'Why would he leave without finishing the job?'

'The problem is – we can only follow the tracks a short distance.' Jacob pointed to where they stopped. 'Beyond that, the ground gets too hard and rocky to see which direction the vehicle took.'

'This is weird!' Keira jumped from the saddle to check the ground. 'Why would anyone want to drive through the break in the fence?'

'Unless they wanted to sneak onto Black Pearl land without being seen,' Reed suggested.

It was all Keira needed. 'You're right!' she cried. 'The driver snuck in. Dad, you know what this means!'

'Stay calm,' Jacob said. 'Try not to get too worked up.'

'Someone snuck in while we were having lunch,' Keira raced on. 'They drove down into the valley, making sure they stayed out of sight.'

'But why?' her dad asked. 'What reason would they have?'

'To get to the meadow by the back road,' Keira explained. To her it all made perfect sense. 'Dad, there's a thief around. Someone drove down with a trailer while our backs were turned. Someone stole Red Star!'

At the bottom of the Jeep Road, Reed split off from Keira and Jacob and turned for home. 'Let me know what happens,' he told them. 'And I'll give my dad the latest news.'

'Thanks for your help,' Jacob told him. 'Be sure to tell Tom that Keira's horse-thief theory is just that – a theory, nothing more.'

Keira hated it when grown-ups did that – reining you back when you were sure you were right. 'Can I go ahead and tell Mom to call the sheriff?' she asked.

'Tell her what we saw and ask her to wait until I get back. And ask her to fix up a tub of hot herbal solution for Tornado's foot. We need to make sure he doesn't develop a blister.'

So Keira trotted Misty along the meadow track, not caring about the rain or the thunder, not even stopping long enough in the corral to unsaddle her horse. Instead, she ran on into the house. 'Mom, Brooke – someone stole Red Star!' she cried. 'We saw tyre tracks up by Dolphin Rock. A horse thief took my pony!'

Allyson listened carefully. Then she made Keira run through exactly what had happened. 'It's possible,' she admitted. 'But honestly, honey – it's not much evidence to go on.'

'A vehicle came through the break in the fence!' Why couldn't they see it? 'We saw the tracks!'

'It could be someone making an innocent mistake,' Brooke tried to point out. 'A couple of guys out hunting deer. People on a family trip who lost their way.'

Keira felt like she was hitting her head against a wall. 'Why won't anyone listen to me?' she cried, breaking into tears.

Gently her mom took her to one side. 'I know you're hurting,' she murmured. 'Red Star means the world – you'd do anything to get him back safely.'

Keira sobbed. 'I don't want anything bad to happen to him, Mom.'

'I know. Your dad and I will need to talk this through. Meanwhile, we just keep calm and wait.'

'Don't let me lose him,' Keira pleaded between her sobs. 'Help me find him, Mom – please!'

'Number one on the list – we make Tornado comfortable.' Jacob had reached the corral just as the rain was easing. He'd tied the pony to a rail and watched as Allyson dipped his foot into a tub of herbal solution. 'Number two, I make a phone call to Owen Mason to tell him Meredith's pony is lame.'

'Ouch!' Allyson knew this wouldn't be an

easy call. 'He won't be happy.'

None of this mattered to Keira. She'd stopped crying, but her whole body felt drained and tired. 'What about Red Star? Every minute we lose, the thief is getting away!'

'I figure we need to follow up with a few phone calls of our own before we contact the sheriff,' Jacob decided.

'Your dad's right.' Patiently Allyson held Tornado's hoof steady in the warm water. The pony seemed to appreciate it – he stood as good as gold with his foot in the soothing bath. 'I'll call the licensing office to check if there were hunters out this way. They sometimes drive off-trail if they spot a deer.'

'And we need to call Steve Carter out at High

Ridge. He's always home on a Sunday, and any person driving a horse trailer onto the highway would have to pass right by his front gate.'

'Good idea.' Allyson lifted Tornado's hoof and examined the soft tissue underneath. 'No need for any painkiller – this looks fine to me,' she told Jacob.

'So let's leave Brooke to bed Tornado down in the barn and go make those calls,' Jacob told Keira. 'Try to keep an open mind about what happened to Red Star, OK!'

She tried. But every way she looked at it, disaster loomed.

'Sit down and eat,' her mom told her while her dad spoke on the phone to Owen Mason.

'I'm not hungry,' Keira answered, pacing the

kitchen, staring out of the window, hoping every moment to see Red Star return to the corral.

'You should take off your wet jeans,' Brooke reminded her.

Keira hardly heard. She was picturing her pony standing at the gate, mane dripping, eyes begging her to come out and get him dry. But when she

looked in the cold light of day, he wasn't there.

'At least take off your boots,' Allyson insisted.

'Hi, am I speaking to Owen?' Jacob asked on the phone.

Brooke, Allyson and even Keira all tuned in to the conversation.

'Hi, Owen – this is Jacob Lucas. I'm calling about a small problem we have with Tornado – yeah, I'm sorry – he got a stone in his hoof, not a big problem, but right now he's a little lame.'

There was a long pause. Tension rose in the room as Jacob's face grew worried.

'I understand, yes. I had him out on the trail, not in the corral – that's correct.'

Allyson frowned then busied herself making coffee.

Brooke and Keira hung on every word.

'I'm sorry you feel this way,' Jacob went on. 'I hear you, Owen. If that's what you want me to do, I'm happy to drive over – tomorrow, yes. OK, see you then.'

He put down the phone, rubbed his forehead and sighed heavily. 'Owen tells me I had no right to take Tornado out of the corral,' he told his family. 'He blames me entirely for the pony going lame.'

'That's not fair. We always take ponies out onto the trails,' Brooke argued. 'It's part of their re-schooling.'

'But obviously Owen Mason didn't know that.' Allyson realised there was more bad news. 'What else?'

'The Masons are pulling out of the retraining deal,' Jacob said. 'Owen wants me to drive Tornado back to their place early tomorrow morning.'

CHAPTER SEVEN

A whole night passed and Red Star didn't come home.

Keira stayed wide awake, ears tuned to every sound – water running in the creek, the creak of the barn door in the wind and rain, Annie and Misty neighing softly to each other in the meadow.

Twice she got out of bed and crept downstairs to investigate a mystery noise, first taking a flashlight into the yard and waving its yellow beam along the row of feed stalls then later shining it under the trailer parked beyond the corral. Both times she came back to the house disappointed.

At dawn Keira got dressed and came downstairs for good.

Her mom and dad were already in the kitchen, making plans for the day.

'Do you need help taking Tornado back to the Masons' place?' Allyson asked Jacob.

'No, you stay here with the girls,' he replied.

Monday and Tuesday were home-school days for Keira and Brooke. It was only Wednesday through Friday that they took the long bus ride into Sheriton to join their classmates.

'Can we cancel lessons today, Mom?' Keira asked. 'I can't think of anything except finding Red

Star!' All night she'd racked her brains, running through all the possibilities time after time and always coming back to the idea that someone had stolen her beautiful pony. 'I've been thinking – who would take him? Is it someone who knows how talented he is – maybe one of our neighbours, or a kid who has to compete against him next month at the county show?'

'You mean, a rival?' Keira's dad gave this some thought. 'Competition does get pretty intense, even at junior level.'

'Exactly! And Red Star has an awesome reputation. A lot of people would want him out of the contest.'

'But I reckon stealing him is going a little over the top,' Allyson said.

'OK, then – maybe someone saw Red Star and fell in love with him,' Keira went on. She sat at the table without eating the plate of ham and eggs that her mom put in front of her. 'Someone who visited Black Pearl lately – like Meredith Owen for instance.'

Allyson frowned. 'I can't see that. Meredith doesn't strike me as a pushy person – more shy and retiring.'

'But think about it.' Suddenly Keira felt she had another lead. 'Meredith and her dad hate the pony

94

they have. They're going to sell Tornado as soon as we take him back to their place, so they're already looking around for a replacement!'

'That doesn't make them guilty of stealing Red Star,' Allyson pointed out.

Keira turned to her dad. 'Owen Mason said he liked the look of Red Star, remember!'

'Your mom's right – it still doesn't make him a thief.'

Keira hung her head, feeling tears well up and sighing deeply. She only looked up again when Brooke spoke from the kitchen doorway.

'Who has a better idea?' Brooke asked calmly. 'Dad, why not let Keira drive over to the Masons' place with you – at least give her the chance to take a look around?'

While Keira helped load Tornado into the trailer, Brooke called Reed Walters and fixed to meet him at the cattle guard below Dolphin Rock.

'Reed and I will keep on searching,' she promised Keira. 'No one's going to give up until we find Red Star!'

'We'll track him down,' Allyson agreed. 'He can't just vanish.'

But it was a whole afternoon and evening, plus a whole night since Red Star had gone missing, and Keira's nerves were stretched to breaking point. 'I feel so bad!' she told her dad as they led Tornado into the trailer and bolted the door. 'I don't know what to do. Part of me wants to check out the Masons, but part of me wants to stay here with Brooke and carry on looking.'

Jacob decided for her. 'Come with me to Norton County. Drop off Tornado and take a look around – at least then we'll have eliminated one possibility.'

'You don't think the Masons did it?' she quizzed, her stomach churning as she sat next to her dad in the cab.

He started the engine. 'Maybe not,' he said quietly. 'But then again, Owen Mason is a ruthless kind of guy – not my favourite client, that's for sure.'

'So we check him out,' Keira nodded, settling in for the two-hour drive.

As the sun rose over the mountains, Jacob and Keira drove the dirt road past the Carters' place out on to the highway. Jacob waved Steve Carter across and Steve promised that he would look out for Red Star.

'I hope you find him. He's a neat little pony,' he told Keira, leaning in through the cab window and studying her pale, drawn face. 'I always say – there aren't many as classy as him.'

'We know it.' Jacob thanked their neighbour and drove on. 'If Red Star doesn't show up before tonight, I'll call the sheriff's office,' he promised Keira.

Her mouth felt suddenly dry and she swallowed hard. 'That means you agree with me?'

'That he's been stolen?' Her dad stared ahead along the straight, smooth road. 'All I'm saying is – Red Star is worth real money on the competition circuit, so it's definitely an option.'

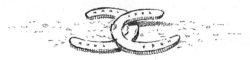

The Masons' house stood at a busy road junction at the base of a steep, wooded hillside. Trucks roared along the highway, but once Jacob turned the trailer down the narrow track leading to the house, the noise died down to a hum. Behind the buildings were a small yard and corral, leading out onto a narrow meadow.

Jacob eased the trailer between tall wooden gate posts into the yard. To his and Keira's surprise, no one came to the front porch to greet them.

'Maybe no one's home,' Jacob suggested, jumping down from the cab.

But Keira pointed to Owen Mason's red SUV parked behind the house. Then she looked up and

saw Meredith at a bedroom window. She raised a hand to wave hello, but the girl stepped quickly out of sight.

Jacob shrugged. 'We're here now, so let's get Tornado out of the trailer.'

Keira agreed. The sooner she checked things out here the better. 'I'll open the corral gate – you can lead him out.'

So they unbolted the back door and Jacob went in to untie the pony.

Keira heard Tornado stamp and snort – a sign

that he was under pressure after the long journey. Sure enough, he appeared beside Jacob with ears flattened and nostrils flared, with dark patches of sweat across his withers.

'Easy, boy.' Keira took the lead rope and coaxed

him out of the trailer. She stroked his neck then led him into the corral, where he lowered his head to sniff the ground. Keira unbuckled the head collar and slipped it off. Taking a second glance at the house, she glimpsed Meredith back at the same upstairs window.

And then Owen Mason appeared from a run-down outbuilding between the corral and the field. He was careful to close the door and lock it before he walked towards Jacob and Keira. Straight away Keira longed to see inside that shack.

Mason cast a glance over Tornado from a distance. 'Is the pony still lame?' he asked.

'No,' Jacob replied, equally brusque. 'We tubbed the hoof and bathed the bruise. He's good.'

Keira only half listened. She was more interested

in the locked outbuilding and Tornado's behaviour. The paint pony sniffed the ground then walked to the corner of the corral where he sniffed again.

Keira followed him. 'Fresh horse manure!' A pile of droppings lay there, plain to see. 'Where did that come from?' she said to herself.

Uneasy, Tornado raised his head and gave a shrill neigh.

'I hope you don't expect me to pay your fee,' Mason was warning Jacob. 'And you'll receive a bill from my veterinarian, once I get him to check the pony.'

Jacob frowned but didn't argue. 'I'm sorry it didn't work out.'

Tornado neighed again and this time a second pony answered from the outbuilding – a high, nervous call from a trapped animal.

The sound passed through Keira like a jolt of electricity.

'No problem,' Mason told Jacob. 'As you can hear – I already bought Meredith another pony. Tornado's heading for the sale barn – he's history.'

Keira didn't stop to think – she ran to the door of the feed store and tugged at the bolt. Mason got there a couple of seconds later and roughly pushed her aside. 'What the …? You quit that, you hear!'

'I want to see inside,' she gasped. 'You have to let me!'

By now, Meredith was out in the yard, not saying anything, only staring at Keira for daring to confront her dad.

'It's my business what I keep in that feed store. I

don't have to let you do anything I don't want you to do,' Mason told Keira.

She broke away and ran towards Meredith. 'That's Red Star in there – that's my pony!' she yelled.

Shaking her head, Meredith backed off.

Keira sprinted back to Owen Mason. 'You have to open the door!' she pleaded. 'Open it and let me see!'

He looked at her through narrowed eyes. 'No way,' he said, turning to Jacob. 'And if you know what's good for you, you'll drag your crazy kid back into that trailer and get out of here as fast as you can.'

CHAPTER EIGHT

'Call the sheriff!' Keira pleaded with her mom on the porch at Black Pearl Ranch.

For two hours on the drive home she'd put the same pressure on her dad. 'The Masons have got Red Star. We have to call the cops!'

Now Allyson tried to steady her. 'OK, so we know they have a pony hidden away – according to your father, Owen Mason admitted as much. But he's saying he bought it, all fair and above board.'

'Then why would they hide him?' Keira demanded. 'Why was Meredith sneaking around the place? And why wouldn't Owen Mason let me see inside the shack?'

Allyson sighed and turned to Jacob. 'What do you think, honey? Is it time to call in the cops?'

Keira's dad paced the porch. 'I say yes,' he announced at last. 'This has been going on more than twenty-four hours – even if Keira's suspicions are wrong, we need to spread the search.'

At last! Keira's heart skipped a beat. Once the sheriff was on the case, he would be bound to follow up the lead to Norton County and the Masons' place. With luck, Red Star would be home before nightfall!

'I'm going to send my school buddies an e-mail,'

she told her parents. 'Get them up to speed with what's happening!'

So she dashed upstairs, looking out of her bedroom window and feeling another jolt of excitement as she took in the view of the meadow with the brood mares and their foals. *Red Star is coming home!* she promised them. *It won't be long now!*

She sat down at her computer, ready to send her e-mail, checking her inbox before she began to type. *Huh!* She read an address she didn't recognise and the subject – 'Red Star' – then brought the message up on screen. Skipping the content, she read the name Meredith at the bottom. *How come Meredith Mason is writing to me?*

It took her a while to stop her head from spinning

and to concentrate on the message.

Keira stopped reading and frowned. Where was this message going? She didn't understand.

> Hey, Keira,
>
> I know you're shocked, but please read this. I'm sorry I didn't say hi when you brought Tornado back earlier today, but honestly I couldn't face visitors – I hate that Dad has fixed on selling my pony without even asking me. I was crying all last night.

Keira gasped. Her eyes went fuzzy as she tried to steady herself and read on.

> After he decided to sell Tornado, he went straight to the sale barn and bought a new pony – did he tell you?
>
> Again he did this without telling me. The new pony is called Diamond – a sorrel with a white star on her forehead. She's sweet, but I still want to keep Tornado, even if he's hard to for me to ride.
>
> So anyway, I wanted to say thanks for working with Tornado and to tell you no way is it your dad's fault.

Everything is down to me – I'm a lousy rider – I need a good trainer, and I'm learning it the hard way!

Anyhow, Diamond has to stay in the store because she went lame in the trailer on the way home from the sale barn. I'm sending you an attachment with a picture of her. Cute, huh? But I still love Tornado better. Maybe I can work on Dad and get him to change his mind.

Quickly Keira brought up the attachment on screen. She stared at a photo of a sweet sorrel pony with a long brown mane and a white star. 'So that's

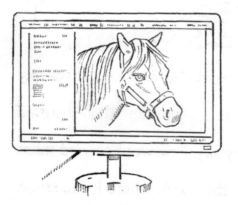

who was in the barn!' she gasped out loud.

She sat without moving, while her theory crumbled to nothing. Owen Mason hadn't stolen Red Star –

Meredith's e-mail and Diamond's picture proved it. Red Star had vanished into thin air and Keira was back to square one.

At last she went to the window and stared out at storm clouds gathering over the vast range of the Black Pearl Mountains. 'Red Star, where are you?' she murmured.

Her lips trembled and tears ran slowly down her cheeks.

As dusk arrived, the temperature dropped sharply and snow began to fall. Large white flakes drifted down from a dull grey sky. The wind carried them in swirling gusts onto the porch where Keira stood waiting for Brooke and Reed to ride into sight.

When she saw them walking slowly along the Jeep Road, she put on a jacket and ran to meet them.

'Nothing. No sign,' Brooke reported glumly.

'We searched National Forest territory way out as far as Sharman Lake,' Reed told Keira. 'When it looked like snow, we headed back.'

Keira hung her head in despair. If Red Star was out there in the wilderness, how would he survive a snowstorm? She knew horses easily froze to death if they couldn't find shelter. And what about food? What would Red Star eat in the snow?

'Come on.' Reed made her walk alongside him and Duke as they headed home. 'I'm leaving Duke at your place overnight. I'll call my dad to drive me back to Three Horseshoes.'

'Owen Mason didn't steal Red Star,' Keira

admitted to Brooke as she walked. 'But at least Mom and Dad agreed to call the sheriff.'

'Sheriff Atwood won't do much until the snow stops,' Reed warned. It was coming down heavily now and settling fast. 'Hey – no need to call Dad – his car is here already.'

It turned out that Tom Walters had thought ahead and realised that his son would need help to get home. So he was drinking coffee with Allyson and Jacob when Keira, Brooke and Reed arrived.

'Are your horses fed and watered?' Jacob asked Reed and Brooke.

She nodded. 'We left them safe and warm in the barn with the others.'

'Yeah, no way can we leave them out on a night like this.' As soon as the words were out of his mouth, Jacob wished he hadn't said them. He gave Keira a quick hug. 'Sorry, honey – but we have to hope that Red Star found shelter, wherever he is.'

'Hey, and listen – I've been thinking,' Tom interrupted. He warmed his large hands around the mug of coffee that Allyson handed to him. 'I was running through in my mind the people I saw hanging around our place yesterday morning – just before your pony vanished.'

'And?' Suddenly Keira felt a spark of hope. She waited eagerly for Reed's dad to say more.

'Well, a couple of Jeeps drove by – nothing unusual in that. They were hunters out for a day's sport. Plus I saw Matt Brown driving his hay wagon up towards Dolphin Rock.'

'What's wrong with that?' Allyson asked.

'It was Sunday. Matt doesn't work Sundays. And the wagon was empty.'

There was silence in the room while everyone thought this through.

'I don't know much about Matt. Where does he live?' Jacob asked.

'Over by Sharman Lake,' Tom told them.

'So maybe he was taking a short cut by Dolphin Rock.' Allyson closed the subject. 'We have no idea what he was doing there, and I don't want you racing away with another crazy idea,' she warned Keira.

'Sorry.' Tom saw he had spoken out of turn. 'But think about those two Jeeps and the hunter guys,' he reminded Allyson and Jacob. 'They had out-of-state number plates – Lord knows who they were!'

'How long has Matt Brown lived by Sharman Lake?' Keira asked Brooke.

The girls were in their pyjamas, sitting cross-legged on Brooke's bed and talking quietly so their mom and dad didn't hear.

Through Brooke's window they could see the moon and a million bright stars. The distant mountains glistened white with a light covering of snow.

'A couple of months. He took over the hay supply business from Luke Thorpe.' Brooke thought hard. 'He has a wife and a daughter. The kid is called Carly. She goes to school with Mylene Carter. That's all I know.'

'So we call Mylene!' Keira insisted. OK, so it was late, but this was an emergency. 'Say it's important!'

So Brooke picked up her mobile phone and called Dan Carter's daughter, quickly explaining what they wanted. Then she pressed the speaker-phone button and handed the mobile over to Keira.

'Hey, Keira, I'm sorry about Red Star. Dad told me about him going missing.' Mylene sounded genuine. 'You want to ask me about Carly Brown. Go ahead.'

'Do you know her? What is she like?' Keira's questions spilled out. 'Does she ride? Does she have her own pony?'

'Whoa – hold up!' Mylene laughed. 'I know her through school. The family came here from Michigan. She seems OK – maybe a little pushy.

And yeah, she rides a pony called Columbine – he's a blue roan. She's talks about him non-stop.'

Keira nodded at each answer. 'What else?' she begged. 'Come on, Mylene, please tell us everything you know!'

'I know this – Carly entered Columbine into the Sheriton show,' Mylene told them. 'Watch out, Keira – she's aiming to become junior reining champion, like she was in the town they lived in before.'

The answer made Keira's heart beat faster. It was exactly what she wanted to hear!

'Reining champion?' Brooke echoed. 'Mylene, are you sure?'

'Certain. One thing I know about Carly Brown is that she's an excellent rider.'

Keira stared hard at Brooke as Mylene brought the conversation to a close. She tilted her head back and closed her eyes.

'Plus, Matt Brown is one super-pushy dad,' Mylene said. 'His kid is going to be numero uno at Sheriton reining championships, whatever it takes!'

CHAPTER NINE

Keira didn't tell anyone her next plan – not even Brooke.

They'd try to stop me, she thought as she crept downstairs early next morning, before anyone else was up. *They'd say I should wait for Sheriff Atwood to get on the case.*

But in her mind, every minute, every tick of the clock counted.

The sky was still dark grey, the snowy ground a

brilliant white when she tiptoed out of the house and went to fetch her bike from the barn. She wheeled it out into the corral, relieved that Captain, Misty and the others hadn't raised the alarm.

'Hey, guys,' she whispered. 'It's only me!'

And the horses had raised their sleepy heads, blinked and turned away.

So far, so good! Keira set the bike on the Jeep Road

and headed out. For once she was glad that the snow was only a couple of centimetres deep – a thin covering that didn't stop her cycling, but enough to give the world a glittery, reflected light. On she went, leaving tyre prints, past the empty meadow, up the slope towards Dolphin Rock.

Halfway up the hill she had to get off and walk, huffing and puffing until the dome-shaped rock came into view. To either side of the track, snow weighed down the branches of the slender aspen trees and footprints of mule deer and coyotes were clear to see.

From Dolphin Rock she had to cut across National Forest land – slopes where redwood pines stood tall and straight and where cycling was hard until she reached another track called Lake Trail.

This dirt road would take her all the way down to Sharman.

The sun was up by the time Keira caught her first glimpse of the lake. It nestled in the valley, shimmering in the low sun's rays. Cycling down the last stretch of Lake Trail, Keira made out a group of buildings clustered by the shore. She headed straight for them, convinced that this was the place where the Brown family lived.

There was a small ranch-style house and a large barn, plus a bunkhouse and other outbuildings. Keira left her bike propped against the bunkhouse wall, keeping a wary eye on the main house. She was relieved to see that there was no sign of life.

When she spotted an empty hay wagon parked beside the barn she knew she was in the right place. Then she heard the unmistakable sound of a pony snickering from inside the barn.

'I'm coming, Red Star!' she whispered, holding her breath and lifting the latch on the barn door. She stepped inside, having to wait for her eyes to get used to the dim light. The sweet smell of hay hit her – there were bales stacked to the roof, and right at the far end of the barn, a stable.

The pony snickered again. Keira ran towards the stable on a wave of hope.

'Oh!' She stopped at the door.

A pony poked her head over the wooden partition – a blue roan with a pure white mane.

'What are you doing?' a voice demanded, and a

tall girl with long dark hair appeared next to her pony. 'You shouldn't be here – this is private property!'

Keira stepped back and stumbled against a stack of bales. She pulled herself upright, her heart thudding, disappointment flooding through her. 'I'm sorry,' she mumbled. 'I thought …'

'Who cares what you thought?' Carly Brown stepped out of Columbine's stable. 'Who are you and why are you sneaking around? Give me a reason why I shouldn't call the cops!'

'Hold it.' Keira was backed up against the stack.

She could hear footsteps crossing the yard. 'My pony went missing a couple of days back. His name's Red Star. I've been looking for him everywhere.'

'So?' Carly blinked. Her jaw was set in a stubborn line and she stared angrily at Keira. 'Is he here? Can you see him?'

'No.' Keira frowned. She turned to see Matt Brown open the barn door and stride towards them. 'Red Star is a strawberry roan. He's about the same height as your pony ...'

'Cut that out!' Matt commanded. 'You heard what Carly said – he's not here.'

The anger in the air made Keira's stomach churn and she struggled for breath. But she wasn't about to give in. 'My pony wouldn't go walkabout,' she insisted. 'Either he's trapped, or someone sneaked in and stole him.'

'OK, I've heard enough!' Matt Brown seized Keira by the arm and began to march her out of the barn. Carly followed hard on their heels. 'I know who you are – you're Keira Lucas – Jacob and Allyson's girl. You don't go around accusing your neighbours of stealing your pony – get it?'

'Yeah, Keira – just because your mom's a famous reining champion, it doesn't give you the right to think you're better than the rest of us, barging in where you're not invited,' Carly cut in.

They were out in the yard, the wind was raising flurries of snow from the top of the hay wagon and a small horse trailer parked half out of sight. A thin woman with dark hair had come out of the house and was watching from the porch.

'I don't reckon I'm better,' Keira protested. 'I just need to find Red Star.'

'You won't find him here,' Matt Brown insisted. He led Keira to her bike and made her pick it up. 'Either you ride out of here or my wife calls the cops.'

Keira had no choice – she had to leave. But something told her that Matt and Carly were lying. They didn't need to act like that, she thought as she cycled away. Like they both had something to hide.

The further she went up the hill away from Sharman Lake, the more certain she grew. *I'm heading back!* she decided after she made it round the first bend. *Let them call the cops – I don't care!*

She waited until she thought the Browns would be back inside their house. *There are places I didn't manage to look,* she told herself, creeping back down the hill on foot. *Those outbuildings, and the hay wagon and trailer.*

But this time she would have to be really careful. No one must see her. She circled the house and approached from a different angle, hiding behind trees and rocks, edging ever closer.

A door banged and she crouched out of sight. She heard footsteps and voices, another door closing, and then silence. After a while she peered out from behind the rock.

She saw that the barn door was closed and the yard was empty. Maybe the Browns were in the house having breakfast – this would give her time to search the outbuildings. Keira broke cover and made a run for the bunkhouse, hid again then edged forward some more.

She'd reached the nearest wooden building and peered inside – there was nothing in there except some pieces of farm machinery. Nor in the next one – only old hay forks, shovels and yard brushes. Keira was running out of options when she reached the hay wagon, eased open the back door and took a quick look.

The wagon was empty, but there were signs that something more than hay had been stored in here. For a start, there was a horse's hay net hanging from a hook, still stuffed with hay. And there was a lead rope and head collar cast to one side in the far corner. Keira took a deep breath then closed the door.

What about the horse trailer? Would the door be unlocked for her to search inside? She reached up and pulled at the handle. The door swung open.

It was dark inside. There was a sudden noise of the house door opening and footsteps on the porch. In a flash, Keira climbed into the trailer and pulled the door closed behind her.

She wasn't alone. The interior of the trailer was

lined with straw and straight away she knew she was sharing the warm, dark space with a living, breathing creature – something large and scared, which only gradually took shape as her eyes adjusted to the darkness.

The animal stood tethered to a rail. His head was raised, ears flattened.

'Red Star?' Keira let out a deep, sighing breath.

The pony recognised her voice. He stretched his head towards her.

'It's me!' she whispered as the footsteps reached the trailer and someone climbed into the cab. 'But is it really you? Red Star, did I finally find you?'

Her pony snorted gently, begging to be stroked. She moved towards him and threw both arms around his neck, burying her face in his tangled mane.

More footsteps approached. 'Dad, why not wait a while?' Carly Brown's voice asked. 'We need to be sure Keira Lucas isn't still hanging around.'

'The sooner I get this pony off our land the better,' Matt replied from the cab. 'I was only waiting for the guy to come out and fix the brakes on the trailer, which he did last night. Now we're out of here.'

Inside the trailer, Keira held on to Red Star and prayed that no one would think to check on him before they set off.

'But Dad...' Keira's unexpected visit had upset Carly. 'I'm scared she's still spying on us. What if we get found out?'

'We won't if I get the pony out of here,' Matt explained. 'Sunday was the worst time for the trailer to break down, but now it's fixed I plan to drive Red Star out of the state to a sale barn where no one knows him.'

'I hope this works.' Carly still sounded worried and uncertain.

'No sweat,' her dad assured her. 'With luck, I'll get a good price for him.'

Keira swallowed hard. She heard Matt Brown start the engine and felt the trailer lurch into motion. She held tight to the rail where Red Star was tethered. 'It's OK,' she told him softly. 'I'm not going to leave you – not now or ever!'

CHAPTER TEN

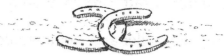

It was dark inside the trailer and there were no windows for Keira to look out of. All she knew was that they were moving fast over rough ground and she and Red Star were getting thrown around.

Matt Brown drove at a crazy speed. He braked hard on bends, honking the horn at anything that crossed his path.

Red Star swayed and staggered. He was tied on a short lead rope, unable to keep his balance as the pony thief made his getaway.

'Easy, boy,' Keira murmured, one hand on his neck, the other clinging to a rail. 'We just have to hang on!'

Sooner or later, Matt Brown would stop. He would open up the trailer and Keira would step out to accuse him of stealing Red Star. There would be witnesses, people who would help.

That was if they survived the journey. Matt drove the trailer into a deep rut by the side of the track – it tilted and threw Keira right across the floor, knocking her head against the wall. Dazed, she slithered down onto the straw bedding.

Matt swung the trailer to the right, revving the engine to pull free of the rut. The wheels spun, the engine whined then the trailer lurched forward.

He's going to kill us! Keira rolled, slid and at last managed to grab the rail once more.

Recklessly, Matt drove on then suddenly braked hard. Keira heard him swear and call out. 'Hey, get those cows off the road!'

There was the sound of cattle mooing and trampling then a voice answered. 'Are you crazy? You could kill someone driving that way!'

It was Reed Walters – Keira recognised his voice. They must have reached Three Horseshoes, which lay on Matt's route to

the highway. Reed and his dad must be herding their cattle from one corral to another.

'Just move the cows!' Matt yelled again. 'And make it snappy.'

'What's the rush?' This time it was Tom Walters' deep, unhurried voice. 'Reed's right, Matt – you were driving way too fast. You spooked our cows big-time.'

Inside the trailer, Keira decided to act. She began to hit her fist against the metal side. 'Reed, Tom – it's me, Keira!'

But the noise of the restless cattle drowned her out and she got no reply.

'Open up!' she cried. 'Please, Reed, open the door!'

From the cab, Matt Brown picked up the sound

of Keira's voice. Panicking, he put the trailer into reverse and backed off towards a fork in the road. 'Thanks for nothing!' he yelled angrily at Tom and Reed.

'Red Star, quick, you've got to help!' Keira left off thumping the side of the trailer and lifted her pony's back foot to show him that he had to kick the metal. 'Like this,' she instructed.

The pony got the message. He raised his leg and kicked hard – once, twice, three times he struck out with his iron shoe.

'Reed, Tom – help!' Keira shouted.

'Hey, who have you got in the trailer?' A suspicious Reed rode Duke alongside the reversing vehicle.

'No one. Mind your own business.' In the

confusion, Matt's foot slipped from the pedal and the engine stalled.

'It's me – Keira. He's got Red Star. Open up!' she yelled at the top of her voice while her pony struck out with his hoof.

Matt Brown swore and jumped down from the cab. He tried to stop Reed from dismounting to investigate, but Tom rode right between them. 'Go ahead, son – open the door,' Tom said calmly.

Keira heard the handle turn, she saw a narrow shaft of light fall across the straw-strewn floor and then sunlight flooded the trailer. Red Star raised his head, bared his teeth and greeted his rescuers with an ear-splitting neigh.

'Nothing but the best,' Keira promised Red Star.

He was back in his stable where he belonged, next door to Annie, across the aisle from Misty and Captain. Keira had tipped a bucket of feed pellets into his manger and he was munching happily.

'From now on I'm not going to let you out of my sight,' Keira told him. 'You hear me?'

Red Star looked up from his feed. He flicked his ears towards her.

'And there's no need for you to worry about Matt Brown any more,' she told him. 'They arrested him and took him into Sheriton. Sheriff Atwood said there's a whole list of unsolved horse thefts they want to look at.'

Red Star gave a snort then carried on eating while Keira watched. Soon Brooke came into

the barn with more news.

'Mom just took a call from Meredith Mason,' she told Keira. 'She says her dad agreed to keep Tornado after all.'

'Cool!' Keira was pleased. 'But what about Diamond?'

'She gets to keep both ponies. From what I hear, Meredith's mom just got back from a business trip. When she heard what had been going on while she was away, she turned right around and said Meredith's dad had acted pretty badly. Firstly, she said they had to pay Dad for the work he did on Tornado.'

'Very cool!' Keira smiled. She felt dog-tired after the day's events but overjoyed at the way things had worked out. She listened to Brooke but didn't for one moment take her eyes off her beloved pony as he crunched his grain.

'Second, Mrs Mason was the one who decided to keep Diamond. She said Tornado was lonely and needed a companion. Also, that Meredith should call Mom and ask for riding lessons.'

The news was enough for Keira to turn away

from Red Star and give Brooke her full attention. 'I so-o-o like Meredith's mom!' she declared.

Brooke nodded and laughed. 'Me too. Meredith said her dad was really moody while her mom was away. Now they're all together and he's not so mean.'

'So Dad gets paid and Mom teaches Meredith. And I get Red Star back!'

'Good day, huh?' Brooke grinned. 'Now all you have to do is put in the work for Sheriton.'

'October 6th,' Keira agreed. 'You hear that, Red Star? It's you and me, buddy, out there in the arena!'

Her beloved pony finished his grain, raised his head and his beautiful dark brown eyes stared straight into Keira's. *So, bring it on – the sliding stops and the flying lead changes, the spinning on a five-cent piece. Let's go!* he seemed to say.

Keira's home is **Black Pearl Ranch**, where she helps train ponies – and lives the dream …

Black Pearl Ponies

Reed Walters' new pony, **Wildflower**, is beautiful but untrained. Keira warns Reed not to push her too hard, but he insists on showing her off at the local rodeo.

Disaster strikes: Wildflower bolts from the arena. Keira and her sister head off into a snowstorm to find her, forgetting the one golden rule – always stick together …

Keira's home is **Black Pearl Ranch**, where she helps train ponies – and lives the dream …

MISS MOLLY

Sable Lucas's parents plan to give her a surprise birthday gift – a beautiful sorrel mare called Miss Molly! They allow Keira's dad three short weeks to train the nervy pony.

Soon Sable is all set to meet Miss Molly, but the great day goes horribly wrong. Why does the pony spook big-time? Keira turns detective to find out.

Keira's home is **Black Pearl Ranch**, where she helps train ponies – and lives the dream …

Black Pearl Ponies

STORMCLOUD

Stormcloud is a crazy ex-rodeo pony that can never be tamed. Or so everyone believes. But Stormy's new owner promises Keira that if she succeeds in re-schooling him and selling him on, she can keep the cash!

Keira jumps at the challenge. Will kindness and patience be enough, or has rodeo cruelty soured Stormy for good?